"Now, you two," Coach Baxter said to Teddy and Sari. "I'm going to give you a chance to prove you can work together. Neither of you will play in the Red Wings game. You will both sit on the bench and watch your team play without you."

I don't think any of us could believe what we were hearing.

Sari and Teddy didn't say anything.

They just sat there with their mouths hanging open.

Teddy and Sari were two of our best players. We didn't have a chance against the Red Wings without them. We were toast!

Well, I thought, *this is it. Things can't get worse.*

"Hi, Mrs. Baxter. Sorry I'm late," a voice called from the end of the rink.

And then we all got our first look at Wayne Wilder, our new goalie.

I was wrong—things could get a lot worse.

The No Stars need all the fans they can get! So don't miss:

#1 STICKING IT OUT

#2 THE PUCK STOPS HERE!

And coming soon:

#3 CALL ME GRETZKY!

#4 LET'S HEAR IT FOR THE SHRUMPS!

2

THE PUCK STOPS HERE!

By Jim O'Connor

•

Bullseye Books
Random House New York

The No Stars™ are created by
Parachute Press, Inc.

Ice hockey equipment provided by **CANSTAR**
Sports, Inc., makers of *BAUER* and *Cooper*
hockey equipment and ice skates.

CONTENTS

Slocum Slumps

1

Any goalie could have stopped that puck. A turtle could have beaten it in a race. It was an easy save.

But not for *our* goalie. Steve Slocum missed that stupid puck by a mile. And a second later the referee shouted out, "Goal!"

Now the Islanders were beating us 4–0.

My name is Mike Beagleman and I play hockey for the North Stars. And we were losing—as usual.

We haven't won a single game this season. That's why the other teams in the

Westside Hockey League call us the No Stars.

I guess we *are* pretty bad. Some of the guys on our team have never played hockey before. Some have never even *skated* before.

But our losing streak isn't all our fault. Lots of crazy things have happened to us this season.

First, the Westside Hockey League put Sari Baxter on our team. A *girl!* The only girl in the whole league!

Next, our coach, Mr. Slocum, fell and broke his leg. Can you believe it? Skating is kind of out of the question for him— since he's in a cast that goes from his toes to his hip. So Sari's mom, Mrs. Baxter, became our new coach.

That's right. A girl on the team and a mom for a coach. That made it pretty hard to concentrate on our game.

But it all turned out okay, I guess. Sari's

a pretty good player—better than most of the guys, actually. And Mrs. Baxter is cool. She knows a lot about hockey. She used to be a professional figure skater. And, boy, can she skate fast! We could all learn a few tricks from Coach B.

And we could sure use them now.

We began playing the Islanders at 7 A.M.

By 7:05, we were down 2–0.

At 7:15, the score was 4–0.

Usually, we don't get four goals down until the *second* period. We were definitely headed to the Hall of Fame—for losers.

The Islanders called a time-out.

"What's wrong with the Sieve?" Teddy Ryan asked me on the bench. Everyone on the team calls Steve that because he lets so many pucks get through.

"I don't know," I said. "He's playing worse than usual."

"Much worse," Teddy agreed.

Teddy and I agree on most things. He's my best friend. We go to different schools, but we've played together on the North Stars for three years. And we even went to hockey camp together last summer.

"Steve's let every shot get by him," I said. "Maybe it's too early in the morning for him. Maybe he's still asleep."

"Well, he'd better wake up," Teddy said. "And fast. My baby sister could have stopped that last puck."

"Hey! Guys!" Felipe Perez skated over to us. "What's with the Sieve? He's not even *trying*."

Felipe is the best all-around player on the North Stars. Usually he plays defense with me or Cliff Parkes.

Last year, Felipe scored six goals in sixteen games. On most teams, that stinks. But on the North Stars, that made him our best scorer.

"I think I can give Steve a few tips. To

get him out of his slump," Teddy said, glancing across the rink. Then he took off down the ice.

"Uh, Teddy. Wait! Wait!" I shouted. Too late. He was already halfway across the rink.

Teddy has a bad habit of giving us lots of advice. Even when we don't want it.

Ten seconds later, Teddy was back. He had a strange look on his face.

"So what did the Sieve say?" Felipe asked Teddy.

"He was acting *really* weird," Teddy answered. "He just kept repeating the same thing over and over again."

"What? What did he say?" I asked.

"'I hate hockey. I hate hockey. I hate hockey,'" Teddy answered.

The ref's whistle blew.

Time-out was over.

We had to get back to the game.

Playing four goals down.

With a goalie who, we just found out, hated hockey.

Go for the Goal!

Coach B. sent our first line back out on the ice. Sari at center, Randy Fernandez on left wing, and Tommy Feldman on the right. It was a strong lineup.

Well, it should have been.

Sari won the face-off. She flipped the puck over to Randy. Randy took it down to the Islanders' end of the rink. He glanced at the Islanders' monster goalie and passed the puck back to Sari. She passed it back to Randy.

No one took a shot!

After two minutes of this back-and-forth

stuff, Coach B. got fed up.

"Okay, second line on the ice," she yelled.

I watched Teddy, Peter Lomenzo, and Lucas Wilson climb over the boards and skate into position.

Lucas used to be one of our best players, but this year he hasn't played very well. His mom and dad are getting a divorce. He's taking it pretty badly. He hardly ever smiles anymore.

And he's been getting a lot of dumb fouls lately—because he keeps losing his temper. The other teams know how easy it is to make him angry. So they pick on him. That way, they can have an extra player on the ice while he sits in the penalty box.

"Hey, Lucas," Danny Whelan, one of the Islanders, yelled. "How does it feel to be king of the No Stars?"

That was all it took. Lucas dropped his gloves and grabbed Danny by the mask.

The referees broke up the fight quickly. Fighting is not allowed in our league. It's a strict rule. The refs gave Lucas a five-minute penalty. That's called "getting a major."

If you get a major, you also get kicked out of the game. So Lucas couldn't play anymore today.

And it also meant we had only five guys on the ice for the next five minutes. The Islanders would have six. They'd probably score another goal. Maybe more.

Coach B. called time out.

"Okay. I want everyone to *calm down*." Her bright blue eyes flashed. "You guys know you *never* fight, and you *never, ever* grab anyone's face mask."

Lucas sat on the bench looking miserable. He ran his hand through his straight blond hair. I felt sorry for him. But he did do a pretty stupid thing.

"With Lucas out, we have to rearrange

our lines," Coach B. said. "Teddy, I want you to switch with Sari. She'll play with Peter and Felipe."

"What good is *that* going to do?" Sari asked. "It makes more sense to keep the first line together."

"This isn't the time for questions, Sari!" Coach B. said. "We have to get out there and play. First line, back on the ice!"

Sari tossed her blond hair back and skated away. She's one of our best players. She always centers the first line. Now she was stuck on the second line. Boy, was she mad!

Back out on the ice, Teddy, Randy, and Tommy played well together. Every time the Islanders skated the puck into our end, one of them snagged it and knocked it back down the ice.

With ten seconds left in the penalty, Teddy made his move. He cut between two Islanders and stole their pass. Then he slid the puck over to Tommy.

"Give and go!" he yelled.

Tommy held the puck while Teddy picked up speed.

Then Tommy made a perfect pass!

The puck reached Teddy just as he crossed into the Islanders' zone. He skated with the puck as if it were glued to his stick.

The Islanders were caught by surprise.

Teddy took an awesome shot.

The puck soared.

Goal!

"All right!" Teddy screamed.

We all skated over to him and cheered. I tapped his leg pads with my stick. We call that an "attaboy."

Teddy's goal got us all pumped. We began playing a lot better. Teddy was totally fired up, too.

"Give it to me! Pass it!" he yelled to Randy when he came out for his next shift.

Randy did, and even though Teddy was too far away from the goal to shoot, he took a shot anyway. The puck bounced off an Islander's skate—and into the net! Goal!

What a lucky score!

Teddy was so happy he danced right in the middle of the rink. He held his stick over his hockey helmet and kind of wiggled his hips.

After that, there was no stopping him. When he wasn't yelling for the puck, he was telling the rest of us how to play.

"Mike!" he shouted to me. "Shoot low. Their goalie can't stop low shots. Tell Cliff, too!"

Then he started coaching Sari. "Don't pass so much, Sari. Go for the goal!"

That's all we heard for the rest of the game. "Go for the goal! Go for the goal!" Teddy's my best friend, but I was getting sick of hearing him order us around.

So was everyone else.

"I sure wish he'd shut up," Cliff complained.

"Yeah, who made *him* the king of hockey?" Sari snapped. "A couple of lucky goals and suddenly he's the expert."

"What do you mean, 'lucky' goals?" Teddy yelled, skating up behind Sari.

"Well, the first goal was good," Sari admitted. "But that second shot was luck. Pure luck!"

"You're just jealous." Teddy glared at Sari. Then he skated back into the game.

The Islanders were way ahead of us now, 12–2. Steve hadn't blocked a single puck yet.

Randy took a shot on goal. It was a hard blast that landed right in front of the Islanders' net. Teddy raced for the rebound. He poked the puck in. Goal!

Three goals for Teddy in one game! Wow! That's called a "hat trick." It's a pretty big deal, we had to admit. We went crazy! Coach B. even took off the Maine Hockey baseball cap she always wears and threw it on the ice.

Teddy skated all the way around the rink. He acted as if he had scored the winning goal in the Olympics.

"A hat trick! Do you believe it?" he yelled when he came off the ice.

"That was awesome!" I told him. But even with his goal, we were still behind 12-3.

And that was the final score.

After the game, we headed to the locker room to change. No one spoke. Except Teddy. He was still pumped up. Giving advice to everyone.

"I know *just* what your problem is—" Teddy started to say to Steve.

But Steve cut him off. "No, you don't," Steve said, shoving his skates and uniform into his equipment bag.

He headed for the door.

He glanced around the locker room.

Then he left with two final words. *"I quit!"*

Like Father, Like Son

Do you think he meant it?" Felipe asked. "Do you think Steve's really quitting?"

"Um. I think he really did," I said. "He told Teddy during the game that he *hated* hockey."

"How could he hate hockey?" Tommy asked. "He's been playing for three years. It doesn't make sense."

"I don't think he hates hockey," Cliff said. "He's probably just tired—from all those pucks bouncing off his head. I bet he'll be back."

"Yeah," Lucas agreed. "Steve will be back."

"Well, *if* he comes back, it would be a good idea if certain people didn't give him any more *tips* about playing better," Sari said loudly. She stared right at Teddy.

Teddy's eyes blinked like crazy behind his glasses. That meant he was about to explode.

"Who asked for your opinion?" Teddy yelled.

That started a really big argument. Teddy and Sari screamed at each other. They were still screaming when Felipe, Lucas, and I left the rink.

"So, do you think Steve will be back?" Felipe asked as we walked home.

"Definitely," I replied, moving my bag of hockey gear to my other shoulder. All those pads and my skates were heavy. "He's just trying to scare us. There's no way Steve would really quit."

"Yeah," Lucas agreed. He pushed a puck along the sidewalk with his stick as we walked. "You can't quit hockey in Monroeville!"

Felipe and I nodded. Almost every kid in our town plays hockey. It's all we ever talk about. After hockey ends, we play on in-line skates. And during summer vacation, some of us even go to ice hockey camp in Minnesota.

By the time we reached my house, Felipe, Lucas, and I were sure of one thing—no way was Steve quitting.

"Hey, what's up?" I asked Randy and Teddy. I had just arrived at the rink for our next game, against the Oilers.

Randy and Teddy sat on the bench with their heads in their hands.

Felipe paced back and forth in front of them. Which is tough to do on skates.

Something was definitely wrong.

"It's Steve," Teddy said, glancing up. "He really did quit."

"Oh, no," I groaned.

"It has to do with love," Randy said.

"Love? What are you talking about?" I asked.

"Steve told Coach B. that he doesn't *love* hockey," Felipe answered. "He *hates* it. He only played because his dad wanted him to."

"When his dad had to quit because he broke his leg, Steve finally told him how he really felt," Randy continued. "Mr. Slocum wanted him to finish the season. But I guess Steve just couldn't take it anymore."

"Hey! Nice move, Teddy," Sari called over to the bench. "You coached Steve right off the team!"

"North Stars!" Coach B. interrupted. "Stop arguing. Let's get ready to play. Brendan, you're in goal tonight."

Brendan Murphy was our other goalie.

He didn't play very often. I guess that was because Steve never missed a game.

When Brendan heard his name, he shot up in his seat. His freckled face turned really white.

"Brendan, are you ready?" Coach B. asked.

Brendan opened his mouth to answer—and threw up!

Randy practically flew to the other end of the bench. All the other guys scattered.

"Brendan, are you sick?" Coach B. kneeled in front of him.

Brendan shook his head and mumbled something I couldn't hear.

But Coach B. heard him. She patted him sympathetically on the back.

"Don't worry, Brendan. You'll be fine. Everyone gets a little nervous before their first game."

Brendan nodded—and threw up again.

Oh, great, I thought. Our old goalie

couldn't stop a puck. And our new goalie can't stop throwing up. Great—just great.

Stop the Puke!

We lost, of course.

It wasn't Brendan's fault.

He tried really hard.

And he never threw up *while* he was playing.

Only in the locker room between periods.

No, we didn't lose because of Brendan.

We lost because we only scored twice.

When I arrived at practice the next night, Brendan was already in the bathroom throwing up.

"This is the second time since he got here." Tommy pointed toward the bathroom.

"I thought Brendan was only nervous before a *game,*" I said. "Not practice."

"You know," Sari said thoughtfully, "we don't really need Brendan."

"What do you mean?" Tony Butler, one of our defensemen, asked.

"I know a great goalie. And he doesn't lose his cookies all the time."

"We don't need another goalie," Teddy said. "Brendan will be fine once he gets used to playing."

"Who's the goalie?" Tony asked.

"His name is Wayne Wilder," Sari answered. "He lives in the apartment next to me."

"How do you know he's any good?" Felipe wanted to know.

"Because he plays goalie for me when I practice at home. We set up a street hockey net and I shoot at him. He can stop most of my shots."

"Big deal," Teddy said. "Steve the Sieve could stop most of your shots!"

"You better watch it, Teddy. Or I'll..."

"Or what, Sari?" Coach B. said as she walked over to us.

Sari turned bright red. "Nothing," she muttered.

Coach B. glanced up and down the bench. "Where's Brendan? Is he feeling any better?"

"He's in the bathroom," I told her. "I think he's sick."

"I'll go get him. The rest of you—on the ice!"

We all piled out onto the ice.

A few minutes later, Brendan emerged from the bathroom.

I watched him skate out to the net.

He didn't look very happy. His face looked sort of green. He put on his helmet and crouched in front of the goal. Then he tapped the goal post with his stick.

"Okay," he said. "Let's get this over with."

We started with a couple of soft, easy shots to warm Brendan up.

He stopped the first one, but only because Lucas hit it right into his stick. Cliff hit another easy shot, this time to Brendan's left. Brendan didn't move. He let the puck slide right by him.

Sari hit one to his other side. He didn't try to block that shot either. He just stood there, as if he were made of stone.

After about five minutes, he began to relax a little. He started to block some shots. He even kicked a couple out of the way.

When Teddy saw that, he took some hard shots. I guess he wanted to show us that Brendan was okay. One shot hit

Brendan's leg pad with a loud *smack*.

Sari hit the next shot even harder. The puck hit one of the net's metal pipes with a loud clanging sound, and Brendan froze again.

Sari and Teddy started taking harder and harder shots. Trying to show each other up.

Ignoring Brendan.

Coach B. didn't even see what was going on. She was talking to someone who worked at the rink. If she turned around, she would definitely *not* be happy!

Their pucks flew at him. Teddy yelled, "That's a goal!" at the top of his lungs whenever he got one in.

When Sari scored, she'd shout, "One more for the good guys!"

Brendan trembled.

"Come on, guys. Give Brendan a break! Lighten up," Felipe said to them.

"This is *practice*. What are you trying to do?"

"Practice *this*, Felipe," Sari said. Then she hit a slap shot toward the goal.

Teddy hit a real screamer at the same time.

One puck hit the crossbar with a loud *clang!* and then bounced away. The other shot hit Brendan in the face.

I don't know whose shot hit him. It could have been Sari's or it could have been Teddy's. But it made a horrible sound when it bounced off Brendan's plastic face mask.

Brendan fell backward. With a heavy *thud.*

Coach B. quickly turned around and rushed over to the goal.

She helped Brendan sit up.

"I'm all right, Coach. I never even saw it coming."

We all helped Brendan to his feet. Then

he and Coach B. headed down the hall to the locker room.

When the coach returned, she really let Sari and Teddy have it.

"You guys know you aren't supposed to hit slap shots! Brendan could have been hurt—badly!"

"Is he okay, Mom?" Sari asked.

"He's a little shook up," the coach answered. "I called his mom and she's coming to take him home. He should be fine."

"I'm really sorry, Coach," Teddy apologized. His voice wavered a little. Brendan goes to his school. They've been friends since kindergarten.

"I'm sorry, too," Sari said.

"I want both of you to do ten laps around the rink after practice. And if I ever see *anyone* taking slap shots at a goalie, you'll sit out the next game. Maybe the whole season! No matter who you are. Does everyone understand me?"

We all nodded.

It's hard to play without a goalie. We practiced passing drills. We ran some plays. But shooting at an empty net wasn't much fun.

"Look, Mike," Teddy said to me. "There's Brendan's mom. I sure hope she doesn't think *I* hit Brendan."

"Well, you might have," I answered.

"Yeah, I know," Teddy said softly.

Brendan walked out of the locker room. With his equipment bag slung over his shoulder.

Teddy and I watched his mom place her arm around his shoulder.

When they reached the door, Brendan stopped next to a big garbage can.

He lifted his goalie stick, and with a hard shove, stuffed it into the trash.

Uh-oh, I thought.

We needed a new goalie.

Again.

The Empty Net

5

"I still think it was Sari's puck that hit Brendan," Teddy insisted.

We were at the Monroeville Mall. In a store called the Hockey Hut.

"It could have been your puck," I said, lifting a stick out of the display. "Both of you shot at the same time."

"No. I'm sure it was Sari's," Teddy declared. "Hurry up. Buy that stick so we can go to the video arcade."

When we reached the cash register, I couldn't believe who was there. Brendan! Buying a new stick!

Maybe we didn't need a new goalie after all!

"Yo, Brendan," I said. "You okay?"

"Uh, sure, Mike," Brendan said with a nervous smile. "My mask saved me."

"What are you buying?" Teddy asked. "A new stick? But I saw you throw the other one away. Was it split or something?"

"Yeah. I'm getting a new stick," Brendan said. "And new gloves, too." He reached into the shopping bag and pulled out a brand-new pair of black hockey gloves.

"Hey, those are the wrong gloves!" Teddy stared at Brendan's hands.

Brendan was buying regular hockey gloves. Just like the ones Teddy and I wear. Not goalie gloves.

"You're not playing goalie anymore?" I asked.

Brendan stared down at the floor. "Um, no. I can't..." he started to explain. "I mean,

I'm just too scared. All the time! My mom and I talked about it yesterday at the rink. I'm just not cut out to be a goalie. Besides, I'm sick of throwing up so much!"

"Does Coach B. know what you're doing?" I asked.

"Uh-huh," Brendan answered. "I called her this morning. I told her I couldn't do it anymore. She was really cool about it. Are you guys mad at me?"

"Nah, it's okay," Teddy said. "Are you mad at me? For taking that stupid shot? Is that the real reason you're quitting goalie?"

"No," Brendan said. "No. Really. I never wanted to play goalie. I only did it because my brother Jack played goalie when he was my age."

"Well, I'm glad you're still on our team," I said. "We need all the help we can get!"

Brendan left the store.

I sighed. "So now we're back where we started. No goalie."

"Maybe Coach B. has a plan," Teddy said. "Maybe she'll make Sari play goal. After all, she was the one who hit Brendan."

"You just said *you* did!" I exclaimed.

"Well, I'm not completely sure. It could have been Sari. Come on, let's go to the arcade," Teddy said, changing the subject.

I paid for my stick, and Teddy and I headed into the video arcade. Straight for SpaceWarp—the most awesome video game in the whole place.

Teddy stopped short when he spotted Sari—playing SpaceWarp.

"Hey, Sari," I said. "Can we play next?"

"Sure," she answered. She gave the video game a kick. "I stink at SpaceWarp. I still haven't gotten past the second level."

"We just saw Brendan," Teddy told her. "He's not playing goalie anymore."

"Yeah, my mom told me," Sari said. "She's really mad at me. She thinks it was my shot that hit Brendan. She says that's why he wants to switch to forward."

"He told us that wasn't it. He said he never wanted to play goalie. It scares him," I told Sari. "Besides, I think Teddy was the one who hit him."

"Hey!" Teddy's head whipped around.

Sari smiled. "Anyhow, the good news is that we already have a new goalie. I asked Wayne if he wanted to be a North Star and he said yes!"

"Without even talking to the rest of the team?" Teddy sputtered.

Sari ignored him. She kept talking to me as if Teddy wasn't even there. "Then I called Steve and asked if Wayne could use his equipment. He gave Wayne every-thing—pads, stick, gloves. They're a little big on him. But I think it will be okay."

"This Wayne guy better be good," Teddy snapped.

"He *is* good!" she shot back. "Besides,

do you have a better idea?"

I knew he didn't. But Teddy wasn't going to back down.

"Can this Wayne guy even skate? Playing street hockey isn't the same as..."

"Wayne will be great," Sari interrupted. "He'll be an awesome goalie. Just because he's not one of your buddies doesn't mean he stinks."

"Does Wayne go to our school?" I asked Sari.

"Uh-huh," she replied.

"Then why don't I know him?" I asked.

"Because Wayne's a year younger than us," Sari explained. "He's in the third grade."

"Whoa, whoa, whoa!" Teddy shook his head. "You think your *third-grade pal* can just walk onto our team?" he sneered. "Just like that!"

"He's probably better than most of your fourth-grade pals," Sari said. "Just give him a chance!"

Sari grabbed the rest of her quarters off the SpaceWarp game and marched out of the arcade.

"What a jerk!" Teddy said to me. "How can you stand her?"

I didn't answer Teddy. I was thinking about Wayne.

A third-grader.

Who only played street hockey.

The No Stars were having their usual lousy luck.

I mean, how good could this kid be?

Sticks and Stones

6

How bad could he be?" my dad asked. I had told Dad all about Wayne as we drove to practice. Sometimes we give Felipe or Lucas a ride, but tonight it was just the two of us.

"Well, he's never played in a real game. In fact, tonight is his first practice."

"You guys sure like to do things the hard way," Dad said with a smile.

My dad is one of the North Stars' biggest fans. He never misses a game. Dad sits up in the stands with his "lucky cowbell." He rings it every time one of us scores a goal—which isn't very often.

My dad was even our coach once. He only lasted one practice, though. He wasn't very good. Then we found Coach B.

"Well, good luck with the new goalie, Mike," Dad said when we pulled into the parking lot.

"Thanks. I hope we don't need it," I replied. But somehow, I had a feeling we would.

I jumped out of the car and raced into the rink. Whoever comes to practice last has to skate four extra laps afterward. I hate extra laps.

Sari, Tommy, and Randy were on the ice. They were practicing their passing.

I skated around to get warmed up.

All the rest of the guys showed up in the next five minutes. Everyone but our new goalie.

"Okay, team, listen up," Coach B. said. "Wayne, our new goalie, will be a little late. His mom called me and said they were having trouble finding his skates."

"Figures," muttered Teddy.

"Did you say something, Teddy?" Coach B. asked.

"No," Teddy answered quickly.

"I didn't think so. Okay, I'm going to try something new for our game with the Red Wings."

Coach B. pointed to Lucas. "I want you to play with Sari and Mike."

Then Coach B. turned to Teddy.

"I want you to stay with Randy and Tommy. That's been a good line for us."

"Yes!" Teddy yelled. He slapped high fives with Tommy and Randy.

"Mom—I mean, Coach—I don't get it," Sari said. Her face was all pink and she was blinking a lot. "I played great with Randy and Tommy before Lucas got his penalty. Why can't I go back to the first line now?"

"Because I think this is best for the team," Coach B. said firmly.

"It's not fair," Sari muttered. "It's just not fair."

Coach B. put her new game plan into action. "Let's go out and work on our checking," she ordered. "I want the first line to bring the puck up the rink. The second line tries to take it away. Then switch places."

We skated out onto the ice. Sari tried to reach around Teddy and poke the puck away with her stick. Teddy stuck out his elbow and smacked her square in the face.

I'm sure it was an accident. But I guess Sari didn't think so. She gave Teddy a real hard shove that almost knocked him off his skates.

"That was a cheap shot," he yelled at Sari. He pushed her back. "Too bad you're just a wimpy girl!"

Sari dropped her gloves and grabbed Teddy's jersey.

Then Lucas shoved Randy! Randy wasn't going to stand for that. In a flash, Randy and Lucas were rolling on the ice, trying to pound each other.

Then Teddy's gloves flew off. And he had Sari in a headlock.

Coach B. blew her whistle over and over again. But no one was paying any attention.

"Stop it!" she finally screamed. I never heard anyone yell that loud in my life.

Everyone froze.

Randy sat on top of Lucas.

Sari had just pulled Teddy's shirt over his head.

"You four." Coach B. pointed at Teddy, Sari, Randy, and Lucas. "Off the ice! Sit on those bleachers and don't say one word to anyone. I'll deal with you at the end of practice."

I wondered what Coach B. would do to them. She was really steamed.

Lucas and Randy skated slowly over to the bleachers. But Teddy and Sari raced each other out of the rink. *Those two never quit,* I thought.

They sat far apart.

And from the looks on their faces, I bet they were each plotting revenge.

The rest of us tried to work on some plays, but Wayne still hadn't shown up. So we couldn't practice shooting. And four of our best players were sitting in the stands.

Finally Coach B. blew her whistle. "Sit!" she yelled.

She took a deep breath.

"There is no place on this team for fighting," she said. "I want *everyone* to understand that. You might see it on television. But there will be no fights on any team I coach. And no name-calling. Lucas, after the other day, you should know better."

"Sorry, Coach," Lucas said quietly.

"Now, you two," she said to Teddy and Sari. "I'm going to give you a chance to prove you can work together. Neither of you will play in the Red Wings game. You will both sit on the bench and watch your team play without you. And after that, you'll play together on the second line."

I don't think any of us could believe what we were hearing.

Sari and Teddy didn't say anything.

They just sat there with their mouths hanging open.

Teddy and Sari were two of our best players. We didn't have a chance against the Red Wings without them. We were toast!

Well, I thought, *this is it. Things can't get any worse.*

"Hi, Mrs. Baxter. Sorry I'm late," a voice called from the end of the rink.

"Wayne, glad you made it," Coach B.

said. "Come on over here."

And then we all got our first look at Wayne Wilder, our new goalie.

I was wrong—things could get a lot worse.

Shrimp on Ice

7

Wayne walked toward us slowly.

V-e-r-y s-l-o-w-l-y. In fact, he just sort of inched along.

When he finally made it over to us, we realized Sari hadn't mentioned something.

Something pretty important.

Wayne was short.

Very short.

You could even say he was a shrimp.

He had to be the shortest goalie in the league. Maybe in Wisconsin. Maybe... anywhere.

Wayne was wearing all of Steve's goalie's equipment. But Steve was a fourth-grader. A tall fourth-grader. And Wayne was a very short third-grader.

Steve's leg pads came up to Wayne's hips. The chest protector reached all the way down to his knees. His catching glove looked like a shovel on his left hand. The goalie stick was at least a foot taller than he was.

The helmet wobbled on his head.

"Sorry I'm late," he said. "We couldn't find my skates. I had to borrow my sister's."

Then Wayne lifted one leg.

Teddy gasped. "You've got to be kidding me!"

Wayne was wearing a pair of girl's white figure skates. They even had the little saw things on the toe.

At least they don't have pompoms! I thought.

"I hope you find your *real* skates soon," Lucas said. "Real soon. Otherwise, well, let me put it this way—it's been nice knowing you!"

Wayne laughed. "My sister said everyone would give me a hard time."

I couldn't believe him. He was standing there ready to play. In girls' skates. As if it wasn't weird or anything.

He had guts.

"Okay, guys," Coach B. said. "Let's see if we can save this practice. Wayne, get in goal. Cliff, Mike, and Brendan—I want you guys to help Wayne warm up with some easy shots."

"Okay, Coach," we replied.

We skated over to the goal. And waited for Wayne. As soon as he stepped out onto the ice, he fell down. He grabbed the door to the rink and pulled himself up. He fell down again.

Cliff and I hurried to help him stand.

"Thanks, guys," Wayne said.

Then he took two shaky steps—and stopped.

He couldn't keep his balance. The pads weighed too much.

He swayed forward.

Then backward. Then forward again.

Then he started waving both arms.

But he couldn't save himself.

A second later, he was lying on his back on the ice.

He moved his arms and feet around in little circles. But he couldn't get up. Or even turn over. He looked like a turtle lying on its back.

"Um. Hey, guys. Could someone help me?" he asked.

We skated over to Wayne. Cliff flipped him over on his stomach. Then Brendan and I each grabbed him under an arm.

"One, two, three," I counted, and we stood him up.

He was okay for about thirty seconds. Then he fell again and hit his head on the ice with a loud *clunk!*

"You okay?" I asked.

"Yeah, I guess so," Wayne said. "Can you help me up? I have to get the hang of this."

I had to hand it to the little guy. He was amazingly brave. He wasn't going to let a cracked skull stand in his way of learning the game.

I helped Wayne stand up.

I let go of him slowly. Very slowly.

I held my breath. One puff, and Wayne would probably topple over.

Coach B. skated over to us. "Wayne," she said, "I think that for now you'd better just practice standing."

"Sure thing," Wayne replied.

Practice standing. Can you believe it? Our new goalie had to *practice standing!*

The No Stars are really on a roll now,

I thought. *A roll all the way to the bottom of the heap.*

Wayne, Wayne, Go Away!

Maybe Wayne couldn't skate yet. But he practiced standing for the next fifteen minutes. And he was getting pretty good at it.

Meanwhile the rest of us ran some plays, with Felipe centering the first line. And Brendan, our ex-goalie, played on the second line with Lucas and Tony.

"How you doing, Wayne?" Coach B. called across the ice.

"I'm ready, Coach," he said with determination.

Wayne crouched in front of the net,

holding the big goalie stick in front of him. He held up his catching glove with his left hand.

"Wayne looks weird," Lucas said, skating up to me.

"Of course he looks weird," I said. "We've never had a goalie who stood only three feet tall before."

"No, besides that," Lucas said. "Those pads. They're way too big. And too loose."

"Let's tighten them. Maybe that will help."

Lucas and I tightened Wayne's pads. Cliff helped.

"How does that feel?" Cliff asked.

"Thanks. A lot better," Wayne answered. Then he fell down. "Don't worry, guys," he explained. "I just slipped."

"Of course you slipped," Lucas snapped. "You're standing on ice! If you knew how to skate, you wouldn't keep falling."

"You have something against people

who fall down?" Cliff said with a little smile.

This is Cliff's first year playing hockey, and he's still learning how to skate. And how to stop. Cliff has a lot of trouble stopping. So he falls down a lot.

Wayne got back into position in front of the goal. He hit the ice with his stick.

"Come on, guys!" he yelled. "Take some shots."

"Are you sure you're ready?" Cliff asked.

"Sure. No problem," Wayne answered. He slapped the ice with his stick again.

"You go first," Cliff said to me.

"Nope," I said. "You first." I didn't want to be the one to kill our new goalie.

"No way," Cliff said. He slid the puck toward me.

"I'll do it," Lucas said. He took the puck and skated backward a few feet. "Okay,

Wayne, here we go!"

Lucas hit a nice shot. Not a real hard one that might freak out Wayne. But not a little baby one either.

Wayne brushed the puck away from the goal with his stick.

It was a good move!

Then he fell down.

"I'm okay. I'm getting the hang of this. Really. Just help me up," Wayne yelled to us.

Cliff took the next shot. Wayne tried to kick the puck away with his skate. The next thing we knew, both of Wayne's white figure skates were up in the air. He landed with a *thud*.

This is hopeless, I thought. *Wayne can't play goalie*. Maybe he was okay at street hockey, as Sari said. But he was totally useless on the ice.

We were doomed.

"We have to talk to Coach B.," I told Lucas.

"About Wayne?" he asked.

"Sort of. Wayne stinks. So we have to convince the coach to let Sari and Teddy play. If they don't play, we're going to lose to the Red Wings by the biggest score in the history of hockey."

Lucas did the talking.

"Coach, Teddy and Sari have learned their lesson," he began. "They really have. I *know* they'll get along now."

Coach B. nodded. She wrote on her clipboard while Lucas went on and on.

"Another thing. Remember when I grabbed Danny Whelan's face mask?" Lucas pretended to grab my mask.

Coach B. nodded again. I thought I saw a little smile on her face.

"Well, the refs threw me out for only *part* of that game. And what I did was worse than just fighting."

"And think of Wayne!" I jumped in. "He keeps falling down. He might let in 25 or 30 goals. That would be bad for his confidence."

I glanced at Lucas. He was nodding his head really hard. "Total humiliation," he agreed.

"He might let in the most goals ever recorded in a single game," I added.

"Please, Coach B." Lucas was begging now. "You have to let Teddy and Sari play. For Wayne's sake. You have to."

"Sorry, guys," the coach said, putting down her pen. "It's nice that you're so worried about Wayne's feelings. But Teddy and Sari have a lesson to learn. They are benched until after tomorrow's game."

Lucas and I skated down to the other side of the rink.

Poor Wayne. His first game was going

to be one big disaster.

And poor us. We didn't stand a chance.

Rookie of the Year

9

It was the night of the Red Wings game. And I was nervous. More nervous than usual. So was everyone else. Now I understood why Brendan was always throwing up. I was feeling kind of sick myself.

"How bad do you think it will be?" Felipe asked me.

"Well, we don't have Sari. We don't have Teddy. And we don't have much of a goalie. So I think we're going to get killed."

Coach B. blew her whistle. "Everybody on the ice for warm-ups. Mike, you get Wayne ready."

"Sure, Coach. Where is he?" I asked. I didn't see him anywhere.

"There he is—I think." Tommy pointed down the ice. "What happened? He looks different."

Wayne stepped onto the ice.

Tommy was right.

Wayne did look different. He seemed taller. Steve's pads didn't look too big any-more. They fit just right. And Wayne was actually almost skating. He could move without losing his balance.

Lucas skated next to Wayne. Every so often he would give Wayne a little shove to help him keep going.

"Pretty amazing, huh?" Lucas said when they reached us. He and Wayne both had huge grins on their faces.

"What happened?" Tommy asked.

"I was thinking about Wayne after prac-tice yesterday," Lucas started to explain. "I knew those pads had to be a big part of his problem. They were just too big."

Lucas's smile grew even bigger.

"Then I remembered our other goalie, Brendan. Except for Wayne, he's the shortest guy on the team. His pads had to fit Wayne a lot better. So I called him up and borrowed them."

"Way to go, Lucas!" Felipe said. "Where did you get the shorter stick? Brendan threw his away."

"My mom had it!" Sari said. "She took it out of the trash can the other night. In case Brendan changed his mind."

Wayne kicked up one leg to show us how he could move. He was still wearing his sister's white figure skates! He saw me staring at them.

"Don't worry, Mike. I'll find my hockey skates soon. I promise."

"Okay," I said. "Come on. Coach wants me to warm you up."

Wayne headed for the goal. He really

was skating a lot better.

"Be sure to give Wayne some nice easy shots," Coach B. whispered in my ear. "I want him to go into the game with some confidence."

The Red Wings finished their warm-ups. I had to skate right by their bench. "Hey, Mike," one yelled. "Who sawed your goalie in half?"

"Don't listen to them," I told Wayne when I reached our net. "They're total jerks."

Wayne shrugged his shoulders.

I hit a soft, slow shot at Wayne's stick. Anyone could have stopped it, and Wayne did. Which meant he was already playing better than Steve. A good sign. Then I gave him another easy one.

And he missed it.

"Rats!" he yelled.

"Relax," I told him. "Don't worry. You'll play great." I hoped I sounded encouraging. "Sari told me how good you are at street hockey. This is just the same."

Wayne smiled at me. "Yeah, but more slippery." He knocked the puck out of the net.

"Okay," I said. "Let's try another one." But before I could shoot again, Coach B. called us over to the bench. The game was about to begin.

It took Wayne a long time to skate over to the rest of the team. A real long time.

But at least he didn't fall down.

Things Get Wilder

10

We skated out for the face-off. Felipe was centering for Tommy and Randy. Cliff and I were back on defense. And little Wayne Wilder was standing in our goal.

The Red Wings won the face-off and stormed up the ice. Their captain, Reed McAlister, had the puck. He's one of the fastest skaters in the league.

I have to admit I was thinking about Wayne so much I wasn't paying attention. And McAlister flew by me.

Now the only person between him and

a goal was Wayne. Teeny tiny Wayne.

McAlister took a hard shot about ten feet from the goal. Wayne barely moved. He just snatched the puck right out of the air with his catching glove.

Then he flipped it over to Felipe, who was skating behind our net.

"Nice save!" I yelled.

Felipe tried to pass the puck to Tommy. But one of the Red Wings grabbed it.

I was ready for them this time. So was Cliff. We skated backward, positioning ourselves between the Red Wings and the goal.

Then Cliff lost his balance and fell. As soon as he hit the ice, McAlister passed the puck to the guy Cliff had been guarding.

Wayne tried to get into position to block the shot. But he moved slowly. Real slowly.

The shot was low. The puck headed straight for the corner of the net. Until a girl's white figure skate quickly kicked it away. Another save by Wayne!

That save got Felipe going. Suddenly he was all over the ice. Every time a Red Wing stole the puck, Felipe was in their face.

When Lucas, Brendan, and Peter took their shift, they played just as well. But the Red Wings' goalie was having a good day. He blocked all our shots.

The big surprise was Wayne. He was awesome. He wasn't a very good skater, but he made up for that with guts. He'd try anything to stop that puck.

Sometimes he'd grab it with his catching glove. Sometimes he'd slam it with his stick. Sometimes he would kick it away. And sometimes he would make a move we had never seen before.

"Did Wayne stop that shot with his butt?" Tommy asked me after one amazing save.

"Yep," I answered. "Boy, is he going to be sore later!"

When the horn sounded at the end of the first period, the score was tied, 0–0.

"You guys are doing great," Sari said when we skated over to the bench. "Especially you, Wayne!"

Wayne couldn't stop grinning on the way into the locker room. He was the happiest person I'd ever seen at a hockey game.

"Everyone, listen up," Coach B. said. "That was terrific. You are really playing like a team. Just remember, look for the open man. Then pass to him. And keep the passes short. Good luck—and have fun!"

The second period *was* fun. We played great. Our only problem was that we still couldn't score a goal.

But neither could the Red Wings. Wayne was tough. The Red Wings should have scored at least four times, but somehow Wayne stopped every shot.

They couldn't believe it. They shook their heads in disbelief after every save. Wayne was amazing!

Meanwhile Sari and Teddy began leading cheers from the bench—together! "Let's go, No Stars! Let's go, No Stars!" All the parents joined in. I could hear my dad ringing his lucky cowbell when the cheer ended.

Then they started cheers for each player. Sari stood on one end of the bench and yelled, "Go, Felipe! Go!" And all the parents repeated it.

Then Teddy stood on the other end of the bench and yelled, "Go, Randy! Go!" And all the parents screamed that cheer too.

Sari and Teddy cheered for every kid on the team. They finished with "Go, Coach B.! Go!"

Before we knew it, the second period was over. The score was still tied at 0–0.

I bet the Red Wings are scared, I thought. *They always score. And if we beat them, everyone will remember this game forever. The Red Wings will never live it down.*

Coach B. tried to keep us calm between the second and third periods. We were going crazy. For the first time all year we felt as if we could win a game.

"Don't change anything, guys," she said. "I want the forwards to keep pushing the puck up the ice. If you have a good shot, take it!

"Defense, stay back. Don't get pulled up to their end of the rink. Wayne, you're playing great. Don't change anything," Coach B. instructed.

Then she had us all stand in a circle around her.

"Okay. As loud as you can: 'Let's go, *No*

Stars!' If they want to call us that, no problem! We know we're playing like stars," Coach B. said. "Ready. Set."

"Let's go, No Stars!" we roared. All the Red Wings stared at us. They were definitely scared now! Definitely!

When the third period started, the Red Wings nearly scored right away. They came out playing real tough. Slashing their sticks and trying to shove us around.

One of them knocked Wayne flat on his back just as another Red Wing took a shot. But Wayne stuck his glove up and grabbed the puck anyway.

After that, no one could touch Wayne. He seemed to know where the puck was going before the Red Wings took their shots.

He stopped everything.

But we still weren't having any luck. Sari and Teddy were two of our best players. If they had been in the game, I know we would have scored a lot of goals.

But all they could do was sit on the bench and cheer. And they never stopped cheering. They led all the North Stars parents in another set of "Let's go, No Stars" cheers.

With only ten seconds left in the game, McAlister stole one of our passes and blasted off like a rocket. None of us could catch him.

McAlister hit an awesome shot. High, hard, and straight at Wayne's head.

Anyone else would have ducked and let the puck go in. But Wayne didn't move. The puck hit him square in his face mask and flew off to the side.

Cliff grabbed it and shot it as far up the ice as he could.

Two seconds later, the game ended. We had tied the Red Wings, 0–0.

I jumped on Cliff and we both fell onto the ice. Then Felipe, Tommy, and Randy jumped on top of us. We were laughing and yelling. Then the rest of the team, including Sari and Teddy, came out and jumped on top of everyone else.

Everyone was there but our goalie.

"Where's Wayne? Where is he?" Sari shouted.

"Over there," Teddy said. "Look."

We could see Wayne lying like a turtle on the ice next to the goal.

"Are you okay, Wayne?" Lucas asked.

"Sure. I'm just a little tired," he said. Then he sat up. "But we won, right? I mean, we didn't lose. So that's like winning."

"It sure is, Wayne," Coach B. said. "Tonight a tie is a win. Thanks to you. Here, you deserve this."

Coach B. handed Wayne a puck. "This is the 'prize puck' for today's most valuable player, Wayne Wilder. You kept the No Stars in the game."

Wayne was so happy he couldn't talk. He just stared at that puck.

We all headed into the locker room to collect our stuff. I wanted to get over to Tony's Italian Kitchen as fast as I could. I was starving! I definitely needed a large pizza with extra cheese and pepperoni after this game.

Teddy and Sari stuffed their gear into their bags. They were actually talking to each other. The coach's plan had worked, I guessed. Teddy and Sari were finally getting along.

I guessed wrong.

"The team's high scorer should always be on the first line," I heard Teddy say. "It just makes sense."

"But I played with Tommy and Randy *first*. You never even *asked* to switch!"

"You're just a sore sport," Teddy snarled.

"Am not," Sari shot back.

"Are too!" Teddy replied.

They kept going back and forth like that while the rest of us changed out of our skates. And they argued all the way to Tony's Italian Kitchen.

When they stopped fighting about who should play on what line, they argued about what kind of toppings to have on the pizza!

So the North Stars were a team again. A team with guys who couldn't skate, players who always argued, and a new goalie who could fit in someone's pocket. But we'd won our first game!

Okay, we didn't win. But for the first time, we didn't lose.

Maybe our luck was changing.

Maybe we'd go on to win a championship. And then—

"Yo! Earth to Beagleman!" Sari was staring at me. "Do you want pepperoni on your pizza?"

"Yeah," I said with a smile. "That'll be great!"

Sari's Hockey Tip

NEVER TRY TO CARRY THE PUCK
ALL THE WAY DOWN THE ICE
BY YOURSELF.

You'll almost always lose it to the other team. The best way to move the puck forward is to pass it from player to player. Here are two types of passes:

1. *The Forehand Pass:* Use the forehand pass when you have a clear path to one of your teammates. To make a forehand pass, keep your stick blade on the ice and

sweep the puck toward your teammate. This is the easiest pass to control.

2. *The Flip Pass:* Use the flip pass to send the puck over the sticks of other players. To make a flip pass, get the puck on your blade. Then lift your stick upward—but no more than a foot and a half off the ice—and flip the puck to your teammate. Let your wrists do all the work.

Mike's Hockey Tip

STICKHANDLING MOVE

The *side-to-side dribble* is a stickhandling move. You can carry the puck down the ice and keep the other team from stealing it by doing the *side-to-side dribble!* Here's how it works:

Imagine passing the puck to yourself. Your hockey stick moves left and right as you hit the puck left and right. So when you hit the puck right, bring your stick to the right and hit the puck to the left. And when you hit the puck to the left, bring your stick to the left and hit the puck to the right.

Hit the puck just enough to keep it moving in front of you. Practice the *side-to-side dribble* standing still either on or off the ice. Hit the puck lightly and keep your head up. Then get on the ice and go for a goal!

Wayne's Hockey Tip

GOALIE TIP

There are lots of ways to stop the puck from zooming into the goal. For example, you can stop the puck with your skate, your stick, your glove, or even your leg pad! One very good defensive move is called *The Butterfly.* Here's how to do it:

When you see the puck coming, drop to your knees and bring your leg pads out to the side. Your legs guard the lower corners of the net and your hands guard the top corners of the net—a sure way of keeping the puck out of the goal!

Practice *The Butterfly* in front of a mirror—this will make it easier to do on the ice!

Jim O'Connor is the author of many books for children. Recent titles include *Shadow Ball: The History of the Negro Leagues, Jackie Robinson and the Story of All-Black Baseball, The Ghost in Tent 19,* and *Slime Time,* all published by Random House.

Jim was raised in upstate New York, where he learned to ski and ice-skate at an early age. He never played organized hockey, but he enjoyed playing lots of "disorganized" hockey outdoors during the long, cold winters. Jim's other favorite sport is long-distance running. One of his greatest thrills was finishing the New York City Marathon.

Jim lives in New York City with his wife, Jane, and their sons, Robby and Teddy.

Don't miss the next book in the No Stars series:

#3: Call Me Gretzky!

"**D**id you hear that!" I said to Sari when we got back to our table. "Mr. Haring's trying to *steal* Teddy for the Sharks! He can't do that! I'm sure Teddy told him to forget it."

"I hope you're right," she said. "Teddy looked pretty interested."

"Nah, he was just being polite," I cut in. But I had a sinking feeling in my stomach. What if Sari was right?

"Well, anyhow," I added, "why would Teddy want to switch teams now?"

"Maybe because the Sharks are in first place and always win the Mayor's Cup?" Sari said. "And he could be their star forward and get his picture in the paper?"

Those reasons sounded pretty good when Sari said them out loud. But I couldn't believe Teddy that would drop our team after three years. Even for the Sharks. No way.

"But we're finally playing better. We nearly tied tonight," I said. "And your mom says we'll win a game real soon."

Sari opened her mouth to say something. She always has a quick comeback. But just then Teddy ran over to us.

He had this excited look on his face. The same look he'd had after scoring his fifth goal. I felt the pizza in my stomach turn hard as rock.

"Guess what?" Teddy said, really loud. "Mr. Haring just asked me to play for the Sharks! How cool is *that?*"